Teachers

by Melanie Mitchell

Lerner Publications Company • Minneapolis

Lerner Publications Company
A division of Lerner Publishing Group
241 First Avenue North
Minneapolis, MN 55401 USA

Website address: www.lernerbooks.com

Words in **bold type** are explained in a glossary on page 31.

Library of Congress Cataloging-in-Publication Data

Mitchell, Melanie (Melanie S.)
    Teachers / by Melanie Mitchell.
      p.   cm. — (Pull ahead books)
    Summary: Introduces the many jobs and responsibilities
of grade school teachers.
    Includes index.
    ISBN: 0–8225–1696–9 (lib. bdg. : alk. paper)
    1. Teachers—Juvenile literature. 2. Teaching—Vocational
guidance—Juvenile literature. [1. Teachers. 2. Occupations.]
I. Title. II. Series.
LB1775.M66 2005
371.1—dc22   2003023028

Manufactured in the United States of America
1 2 3 4 5 6 – JR – 10 09 08 07 06 05

"Good morning, boys and girls," says a voice from inside the **classroom.**

Whose voice is it?

It is the voice of the teacher. She is welcoming the children to school.

The teacher is in charge of the
classroom. The children are the
teacher's **students.**

Teachers are important to the
community. Students learn a lot
from teachers.

Teachers help students learn about the world and the people in it. They help students be a part of the community.

Teachers spend most of their time
helping students learn new things.

Teachers teach many subjects.
They teach reading, math, science, art,
and music.

Teachers make the rules for the classroom. They make sure students follow the rules.

Sometimes
teachers have
to talk to students
to remind them of
the classroom
rules.

Shhh! These students are taking a test.

The teacher will grade their tests when
they are done. Grading tests and
papers is part of the teacher's job.

This teacher is busy putting grades on a student's report card.

A report card shows how well a student is doing at school. Teachers send report cards home to students' families.

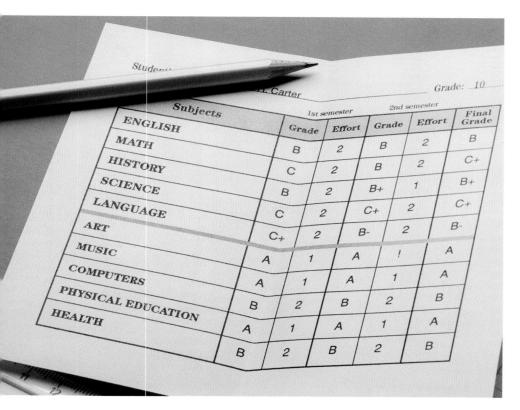

Student: _____ Carter

Grade: 10

Subjects	1st semester		2nd semester		Final Grade
	Grade	Effort	Grade	Effort	
ENGLISH	B	2	B	2	B
MATH	C	2	B	2	C+
HISTORY	B	2	B+	1	B+
SCIENCE	C	2	C+	2	C+
LANGUAGE	C+	2	B-	2	B-
ART	A	1	A	!	A
MUSIC	A	1	A	1	A
COMPUTERS	B	2	B	2	B
PHYSICAL EDUCATION	A	1	A	1	A
HEALTH	B	2	B	2	B

15

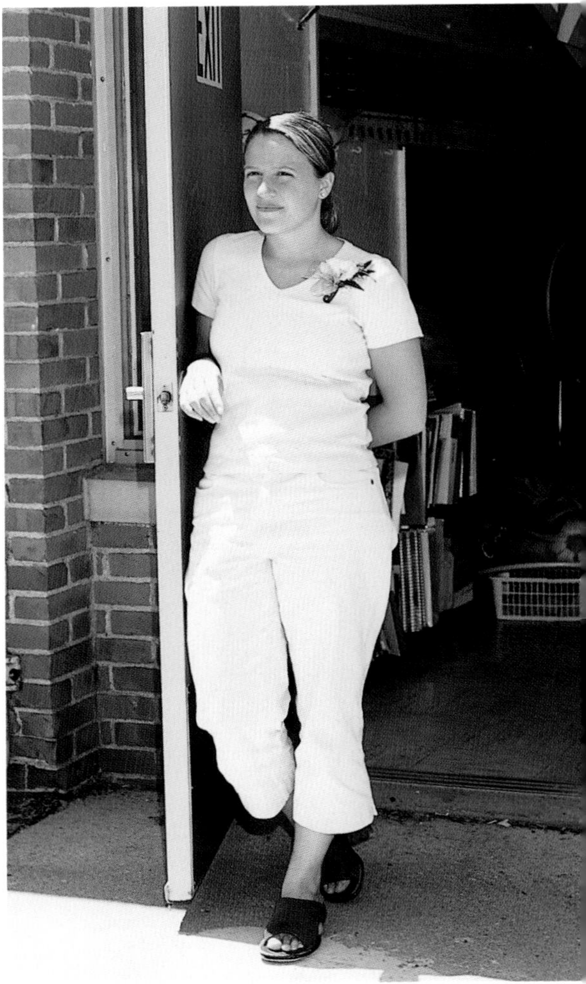

What is this
teacher doing
outside on the
playground?

She is watching the students at
recess. She makes sure everyone
plays fair and no one gets hurt.

Tweet! Tweet! There goes this
teacher's whistle. What is she doing?

She is teaching a gym class. Teachers help students learn how to play sports and games.

Sometimes teachers meet with the
parents of their students.

They talk to the parents about how
their child is doing in school.

Where are these students and their teacher going?

They are going on a **field trip.**
Teachers take students on field trips to
help them learn more. Field trips are
fun too!

The day is almost over. The teacher is
giving students homework.

The students are leaving school. The teacher sees them off safely.

Teachers work before school starts and after school is over. They prepare the classroom and **lessons.**

They also stay after school to finish their work for the day. Good-bye, teacher!

Facts about Teachers

■ Many teachers live near their schools. They are important members of the community. You might have a teacher living in your neighborhood.

■ People train to become teachers. All teachers study **education.** They study how people learn and some of the best ways to teach. Some teachers also study special subjects, such as history and English.

■ Teachers are always learning. Teachers take special classes. They take classes so they can teach their students new things each year.

Teachers through History

Teaching has always been important. But the ways that people teach have changed over the years.

- In ancient Greece, teachers were wise men who spoke to groups of students. Their students were mostly older boys.

- During colonial times in the United States, teachers held school for only a few months each year. Families thought it was more important for children to work at home than to attend school.

- During the 1800s in the United States, teachers taught students of many different ages in one-room schoolhouses.

- Students from rich families were often taught at home in the 1800s. Their teachers would teach all of the children in the family.

More about Teachers

Check out these books and websites about teachers:

Books

Grant, Jim, and Irv Richardson. *What Teachers Do When No One Is Looking.* Peterborough, NH: Crystal Springs Books, 1997.

Hayward, Linda. *A Day in a Life of a Teacher.* New York: Dorling Kindersley Publishing, 2001.

Nelson, Robin. *School Then and Now.* Minneapolis: Lerner Publications Company, 2003.

Weber, Valerie, and Gloria Jenkins. *School in Grandma's Day.* Minneapolis: Carolrhoda Books, Inc., 1999.

Websites

Library of Congress, *America's Story,* "Explore the States." Minnesota: "Remembering the Little Red Schoolhouse." http://www.americaslibrary.gov/cgi-bin/page.cgi/es/mn/schlhse_1

New York: "One-Room Schoolhouse." http://www.americaslibrary.gov/cgi-bin/page.cgi/es/ny/school_1

Only a Teacher
http://www.pbs.org/onlyateacher/

Glossary

classroom: a place where students learn

community: a group of people who live in the same city, town, or neighborhood. People in the same community usually share the same fire department, schools, libraries, and other helpful places.

education: the study of how people learn and the best ways to teach

field trip: a visit or trip outside the classroom. Students and teachers take field trips to museums, zoos, factories, and other special places.

lessons: things learned or studied

playground: a special area where kids can play games or sports

recess: time during the school day for students to rest or play

students: people who study, especially in a school

Index

Photo Acknowledgments

The photographs in this book appear courtesy of: © David Pollack/CORBIS, front cover; © Todd Strand/ Independent Picture Service, pp. 3, 4, 5, 7, 13, 20, 21, 25, 26; © Nana Twumasi/Independent Picture Service, pp. 6, 12, 14, 24; © PhotoDisc Royalty-Free, pp. 8, 23; © Royalty-Free/CORBIS, pp. 9, 15, 22; © Independent Picture Service, pp. 10, 11, 27; © Stephen G. Donaldson, pp. 16, 17, 18, 19; Library of Congress, LC-USZ62-088603, p. 29.